First published in the United States
of America in 1990 by The Mallard Press

Mallard Press and its accompanying design
and logo are trademarks of BDD Promotional
Book Company, Inc.

Produced by
Twin Books
15 Sherwood Place
Greenwich, CT 06830

ISBN 0 792 45404 9

Printed in Hong Kong

Disney's
MICKEY MOUSE
IN
THE VIKING'S EYE

Written by
Nikki Grimes

TWIN BOOKS

MALLARD PRESS

So far, Mickey and Minnie had had a very quiet vacation in Sweden. On their last morning there, they bundled up against the cold and headed for the museum. They were planning to go ice skating later that day, so they had their skates slung over their shoulders. But first they were going to see the *Vasa*, a famous ancient Swedish warship.

As they approached the museum entrance, someone burst through the doors, nearly knocking Mickey down. A guard came tearing out after him.

"Thief! Thief!" yelled the guard. "Stop him!"

"That man has stolen the Viking's Eye!" said the guard.

"Oh, no!" said Minnie. She'd read about this famous jewel, which had been found in the eye of the *Vasa's* largest gargoyle. For years, it had been hidden beneath the mud that had covered the whole ship, but it had recently been uncovered and restored. The Viking's Eye was a priceless gem.

"Mickey, we've got to stop that man!" said Minnie.

"You're right!" agreed Mickey. " Come on!"

The thief ran across the street and pushed his way through a gate. Mickey and Minnie were close behind and saw him disappear around the corner of a bakery. The thief dropped a piece of paper as he ran, but he didn't seem to notice.

Rounding the corner, Minnie saw the slip of paper fluttering to the ground. But the thief had disappeared.

Minnie picked up the slip of paper. "Vasterlang 33," she read, wondering what it meant. She and Mickey went back to the museum and showed the slip of paper to the guard.

"*Ja!*" said the guard. "I know this place! It is the name of a street in the Old Town—building number 33."

Mickey asked the guard for directions to the Old Town, and he and Minnie were soon on their way.

MUSEET

Mickey and Minnie found the address. It was an old apartment house, sandwiched between two antique shops. The door was locked. Mickey paced the cobblestone street, wondering what to do next.

Minnie noticed a cafe across the street. "Let's wait there," she said. "If we sit by the window, we'll see anyone coming in or out of the building."

Mickey smiled. "Good idea, Minnie."

Mickey ordered a sandwich and was just about to bite
into it when Minnie saw someone enter Vasterlang 33.
"It's him!" said Minnie.

Mickey joined her at the door of the cafe, and they waited for the thief to reappear. When he came out of the apartment house a few minutes later, he was wearing a ski outfit. He had a pair of ice skates over his shoulder and snowshoes stuffed under one arm.

The thief hurried off down the long street, heading for the underground train station. Mickey and Minnie followed at a distance, afraid of being spotted. They'd lost him once; they didn't want to lose him again.

The short train ride led to the waterfront, where the thief got off and hurried to a long pier. There were several boats tied up along the pier, including a couple of old steamers. The thief boarded one of these.

Mickey and Minnie hung back and watched the thief meet the boat's captain on deck. Minnie couldn't hear what the thief and the captain were saying, but she did see the captain raise a giant magnifying glass to his eye and lean forward. It looked as if he were studying something on the thief's sweater.

"What's he looking at?" Mickey wondered aloud.

"Us!" gasped Minnie. The captain had straightened up suddenly and was pointing right at them.

On the boat, the thief shouted, "Get this tub movin'!"

"I can't!" said the captain. "The lake's frozen over!"

"Rats!" growled the thief, and he jumped over the side of the boat. He put on a ski mask and snapped on his ice skates, then took off over the icy surface of the lake.

Mickey and Minnie hurried into their own skates.

"I don't like this," said Minnie, mistrusting the frozen lake.

"Look at it this way," said Mickey, laughing. "You wanted to go skating!"

"Very funny!" replied Minnie, as they started after the stranger.

Mickey shouldn't have laughed. Halfway across the lake, he glanced behind him and noticed a rapidly forming zig-zag in the ice, heading in their direction. The ice was breaking up, and he and Minnie still had a long way to go before they reached the shore.

"Faster!" yelled Mickey, grabbing Minnie by the hand. Minnie looked over her shoulder and saw the split in the ice.

"It's getting bigger!" cried Minnie. Quickly, she looked around for a shortcut across the lake. "This way!" she ordered, taking the lead. Mickey was relieved to see the shore come into view.

The thief was way ahead of them, though. They'd have to hurry.

The jewel thief climbed up onto the bank, quickly undid his ice skates and slipped on his snowshoes. He looked back at Mickey and Minnie and sneered, certain they would never catch him now.

Mickey and Minnie finally reached the shore and clambered up onto solid ground, panting.

Mickey and Minnie slumped against a tree. "If only we had some skis," said Mickey, frowning. But they didn't, and it made him angry to think that they had chased the thief all that way, only to lose him now.

"Ouch!" cried Minnie. Something had fallen on her head. She looked down and saw that it was a wide strip of birch bark.

"Hey!" said Mickey, picking up the bark strip. "Help me find more of these, and give me the laces from our ice skates. I've got an idea."

In no time, Mickey had rigged up two pairs of homemade skis. Then he found some sturdy branches they could use as ski poles.

Once their skis were securely fastened, Mickey and Minnie found the thief's snowshoe tracks and followed them. They took extra-long strides to make up for lost time. They were beginning to worry that they'd lost the thief for good when Minnie caught sight of his bright blue ski mask.

Mickey almost ran the distance that separated him from the thief. When he was close enough, Mickey tackled the thief. The two tumbled in the snow and went rolling down the hill.

The thief rose first, shook the snow off, and ran into the forest before Mickey could get to his feet.

Minnie skied over and helped Mickey up. He was a bit dazed by the tumble, but otherwise unhurt. Fortunately, Minnie had kept her eyes on the thief and knew which way he had gone.

"Maybe we can still catch him," said Mickey.

"Well, then," said Minnie with determination, "let's get moving!"

As Mickey and Minnie tracked the thief, they skied by a pair of moose. The big moose snorted a warning, but he allowed Minnie to stop and pet the calf. Suddenly, Mickey realized that it was getting dark and no one knew where they were.

"Minnie," he said, "you'd better go find a policeman. I'll keep after this guy until you get back."

Reluctantly, Minnie agreed.

Mickey was out of breath. He wasn't used to working so hard in the freezing cold. "Maybe the thief will be tired, too," thought Mickey. And he was right.

Just ahead, the thief was leaning against a tree, trying to catch his breath. He had no idea that Mickey was so close. And this time there was nowhere for the thief to run. He had come to another lake, but this one was only frozen in spots.

"Give up!" shouted Mickey, skiing towards the thief. "We know you have the jewel!"

The thief looked up when he heard Mickey's voice.
He made a dash for freedom, trying to hop from one ice
floe to another, but he slipped and fell into the water.
    With no thought for his own safety, Mickey dove into
the icy lake and dragged the thief back to shore.

At that very moment, Minnie and a police officer came speeding up on a snowmobile. The policeman grabbed blankets from the trunk and wrapped them around Mickey and the thief, while Minnie handed them cups of hot chocolate from a thermos.

"Mickey, are you all right?" asked Minnie, worried. Mickey's teeth were chattering so hard he could barely speak, but he managed to answer, "I'm-m-m f-f-f-f-fine, M-m-m-Minnie."

Once Mickey and the thief had recovered, the officer took out his handcuffs and pulled the ski mask up over the thief's face.

"Wild Man Ulf!" declared the policeman. "We've waited a long time to catch you!"

"This man is an international jewel thief, wanted by several countries," the policeman explained to Mickey and Minnie.

"But where is the Viking's Eye?" asked Mickey.

Minnie suddenly remembered the steamboat captain staring at Ulf's chest with the magnifying glass. She smiled and pointed to Ulf's sweater. There, in the center of a giant snowflake pattern, was the Viking's Eye, held in place by a web of thread.

"Well, I'll be darned!" whispered Mickey.

The next day, officials of the national museum called a press conference to announce the safe return of the Viking's Eye. Then, before a huge crowd, the museum guard they'd met earlier handed Mickey and Minnie a crystal sculpture of the *Vasa* itself as a thank-you gift.

Mickey decided to let Minnie have the sculpture. He didn't need anything to remind him of this adventure. He'd remember it every time it snowed!